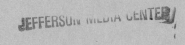

The Pigrates Clean Up

First edition
Published by Henry Holt and Company, Inc.,
115 West 18th Street, New York, New York 10011.
Published simultaneously in Canada by Fitzhenry & Whiteside Ltd.,
91 Granton Drive, Richmond Hill, Ontario L4B 2N5.

Library of Congress Cataloging-in-Publication Data
Kroll, Steven.
The pigrates clean up / Steven Kroll; illustrated by Jeni Bassett.
"A Bill Martin book."
Summary: Pig pirates work hard to get their ship
and themselves clean for their captain's wedding.
ISBN 0-8050-2368-2 (acid-free paper)
[1. Pigs—Fiction. 2. Pirates—Fiction.   3. Cleanliness—Fiction.
4. Stories in rhyme.] I. Bassett, Jeni, ill. II. Title.
PZ8.3.K899Ph   1993
[E]—dc20   92-21823

Printed in the United States of America
on acid-free paper.∞

1 3 5 7 9 10 8 6 4 2

For Jeni, who began it,
and for Abigail
—S. K.

For Steven and Abigail
—J. B.

The Pigrates Clean Up

Steven Kroll ◆ Illustrated by Jeni Bassett

A Bill Martin Book

Henry Holt and Company ◆ New York

We are the jolly pigrates,
We sail the seven seas.
We like to dig for treasure,
We're not too hard to please.

Yo ho, yo ho,
We're always on the go!

Clean-Up Time!

Captain Dan was in distress,
Stamped on deck, said, "What a mess!
Dirty pigrates, do not pout,
There's no time to slouch about.
Look at all this dust and dirt,
None of you has one clean shirt!
And tomorrow, at high tide,
We'll reach shore, you'll meet my bride.
How can Kate and I be wed
If you look like unmade beds?
Grab your mops and grab your pails,
Hurry, scurry, move your tails.
There is lots for us to do
As we clean our ship and you!"

Swabbing the Deck

Puffing pigrates, big and small,
Answered their good captain's call,
Came on deck with mops and pails,
Scrubbed the planks and rubbed the rails,
Mopped the cabins, polished brass,
Washed the wheel and cleaned the glass.
Splashing water, sudsy bubbles,
Soggy sponges, soapy puddles.
There were yards of wood to scour,
They were busy for an hour.
When the ship began to gleam,
It was every pigrate's dream.

Clean Your Room!

Cabin chaos, pigrate slobs!
But they had to do their jobs.

Pigrate Paula put in rows
All her boots and shoes and bows.
Pigrate Sam, in stocking feet,
Straightened out his rumpled sheets.
Pigrate Polly folded clothes,
Handkerchiefs, and pantyhose.
Pigrate Jimmy steamed and pressed
Pantaloons and wrinkled vest.

In their cubbies down below,
Pigrates worked by lantern's glow.
When the call came "Clean your rooms!"
They were hanging up their brooms.

Clean Clothes

First-mate Sarah sounded tough—
Hooves on hips, she'd had enough.
"Filthy pigrates, off you scamper.
Dirty clothes go in the hamper!"

Pigrates lined up in a row,
Washed and bleached and scrubbed to show
Just how clean their clothes could look
For the captain's wedding book.

Polishing Shoes

Pigrate Ed took off his shoe.
He had quite a job to do—
With his fingers and his thumb,
He attacked the chewing gum
Caught between the heel and toe.
Could he ever make it go?

Then with rag and polish, too,
Ed went at his dirty shoe,
Brushed it high and brushed it low,
Till it had a lovely glow.

When he'd placed it in the sun
He took off the other one.

Wash Your Hands
Before You Eat!

Pigrates working, pigrates sweating,
Getting ready for the wedding.
Every one was getting thinner,
They were ready for their dinner.
Mouths hung open, tongues hung out,
When the cook began to shout,
"Wash your hands before you eat
Or you may not have a seat!"
Pigrates trooped out one by one
And they got the washing done.
Their old cook knew what was best,
Even if he was a pest.
Who could blame him in this band
For confusing hoof with hand?

Washing Hair

Pigrates thought it wasn't fair
That they'd have to wash their hair.
But they knew each wedding guest
Had to try and look his best.
They decided what they'd do—
Help each other to shampoo.

Eager pigrates climbed on chairs,
Dumped some water on the hair
Of the pigrates down below,
Keeping up a steady flow,
As they slopped the pink shampoo,
Rubbing, kneading, sticky goo
Into bristly, spiky hair,
Taking extra-special care.

After that they traded places,
Soapsuds on their piggy faces.

Brushing Hair

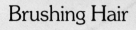

Johnny Pigrate sat and stared
At his hopeless, tangled hair.
It was washed and it was dried,
But it was no source of pride.

No amount of pink shampoo
Or the helpful pigrate crew
Could disguise the awful truth—
Johnny was a lazy youth
Who had just begun to care
That he'd never brushed his hair.

Trying not to break his neck,
Johnny rolled around the deck.
Here and there and round and round,
He was tearing up some ground,
Struggling with his brush and comb
Back and forth across his dome.

So much effort, so much pain,
Inch by inch a little gain.
Hours passed, it grew quite late,
Johnny's hair was nice and straight.

Taking a Bath

Pigrate Sam jumped in the tub—
What a treat to splash and rub—
Soaped his tummy, soaped his ears,
Hadn't been so clean in years.

Sam dove down and swam about,
Blowing bubbles through his snout,
Washed his neck and felt so clever—
He could stay in here forever.

It was fun just getting clean,
But his friends were loud and mean.
"Finish up!" he heard them shout.
"Be a buddy, come on out!"

Pigrates barged right through the door,
Dumped poor Sam out on the floor.

Clipping Nails

Clipping nails is fun to do.
First you must remove your shoe
Or your glove, depending on
Ends of you that must be done.
Then the clipper works its wonders,
Moving all around and under
Every single nail in sight,
Shaping them exactly right.

Pigrate Nate had special clippers
In a case that closed with zippers.
All the pigrates lined up straight
And displayed their hooves for Nate.
Then he mussed and fussed and clipped,
And his clippers never slipped.

Brushing Teeth

Polly Pigrate never would
Brush her teeth the way she should,
So her breath was always foul,
Cavities would make her howl.
But tonight she knew she should
Try to make her teeth look good.

Polly grabbed the dental floss.
"Teeth," she said, "I am the boss!"
Then she worked the floss around,
In and out and up and down,
Till her mouth began to feel
Free of bits of jam and peel.

Squeezing toothpaste, good and thick,
On the toothbrush double quick,
Polly brushed with all her might,
Soon her teeth were shining bright.
"Teeth," she said, "you look so fine,
I'm so glad that you're still mine!"

The Wedding

What a day for Captain Dan,
With his pigrates, spick-and-span,
Out on deck, both tall and short,
As the ship sailed into port.
Searching for his wife to be,
"Yes," said Dan, "I think that's she!"

She was big and she was wide—
Such a perfect pigrate bride!
And she was all dressed in white—
What a perfect pigrate sight!
Every pigrate thrilled to see
What a prize this bride would be!

Captain Dan smiled at her size
And his pigrates' wild surprise.
On the deck he married Kate
With the help of his first mate.
Pigrates in a merry mood
Dug into the piles of food.

We are the jolly pigrates,
We are so clean and bright,
We love to dance at weddings,
We really are a sight!